To Radines

May your life be filled with adventure.

Love
Grandma
Armstrong

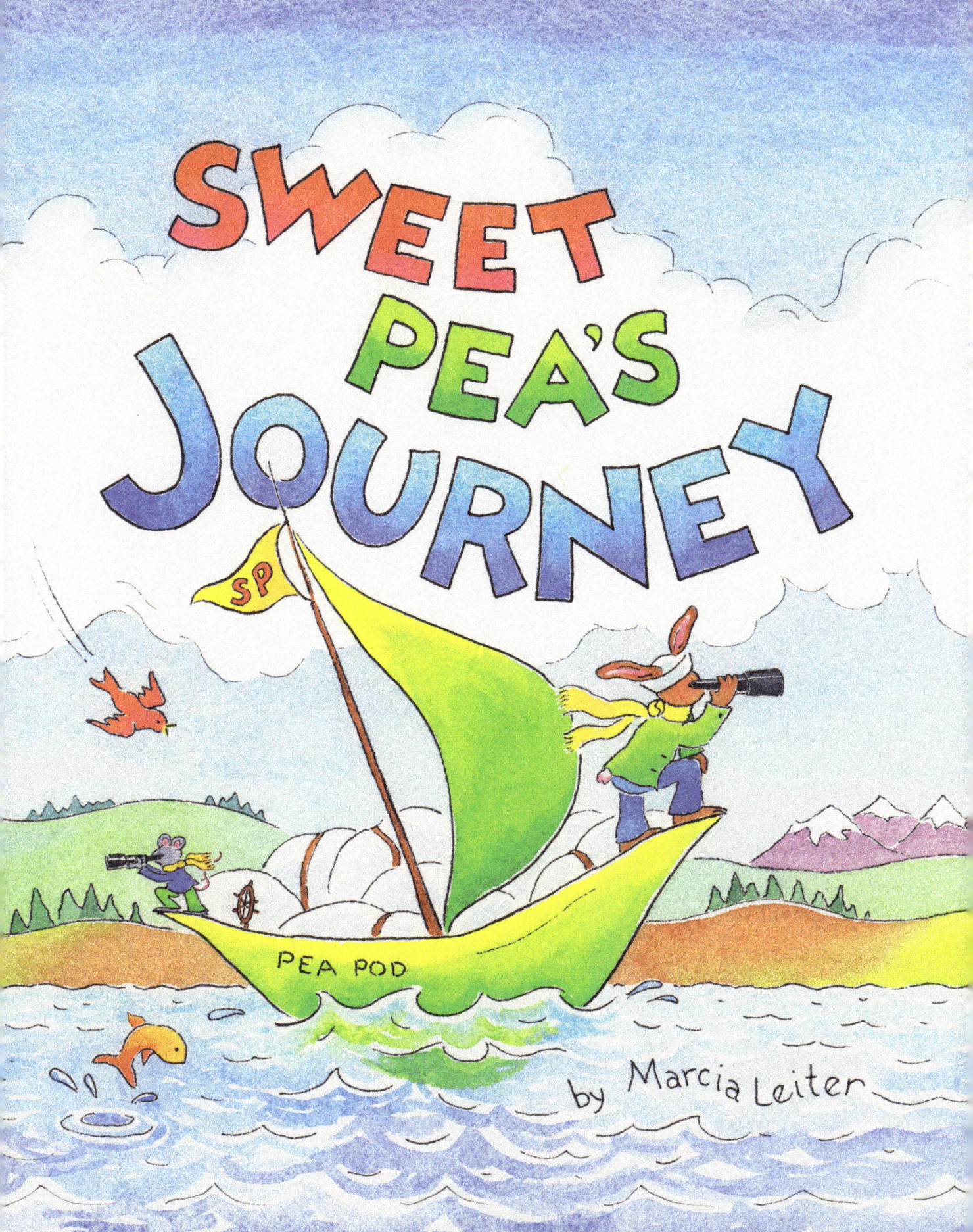

Sweet Pea Tales
Book 3

SWEET PEA'S JOURNEY
Story, Illustrations and Book Design
by Marcia Leiter

Birdberry Press Copyright 2019

ISBN 978-0-9970626-5-6 All rights reserved.
No part of this book may be reproduced or transmitted in any form or by any means, electronic or mechanical, including photocopying, recording, or any information storage and retrieval system, without written permission from the author, except in the case of brief quotations embodied in critical articles and reviews.

Other books by Marcia Leiter:
Sweet Pea's Tale of TOO MANY TOMATOES!
SWEET PEA'S CHRISTMAS

Visit Sweet Pea at
sweet-pea.net

Dedicated to
Ben

who journeyed South
through the Americas
up into the Andes
and down the Amazon.

Sweet Pea was an industrious little bunny
         who lived in a quiet tidy hole by the stream.

But on this particular dreary winter morning
                     her hole was NOT tidy

and Sweet Pea did NOT feel industrious.

There were
  overturned chairs
    half-empty bowls
      broken tea cups
        forgotten mittens
      orange peels
    tiny hats
  cake crumbs
  pine needles
    holly berries
      shredded ribbons
        sticky candy canes
          drippy candles
        stinky socks
      dust bunnies
and muddy, scuzzy
paw prints everywhere.

Then Sweet Pea plopped her boat into the icy black water and paddled away without looking back.

She stopped in Town to pick up a few supplies...

...and sleeping on sweet pine needles under the stars.

It took six days to dry everything out.

Finally Sweet Pea packed up her boat and flopped down on a rock. She dreamed she was a cold, wet FISH.

Then Sweet Pea remembered: "I am an industrious little bunny and I must go SOUTH." She dragged five logs from the woods and tied them together with strips of bark.

All that work made her very very hungry.

That night there were no stars or soft pine needles, just a damp dreary drizzle. Sweet Pea's ears got soggy wet.

In the morning she nibbled some moss then set out again on her raft. It rained for 13 days.

And then it stopped. "This is **better**," said Sweet Pea.

Soon she came to a Big River running right-paw-ways in front of the rising sun.

"SOUTH!" she said.

Her little raft swirled and twirled as it joined the bigger water. Giant boats made giant waves that made Sweet Pea COLD and WET again.

"This will not do!" said Sweet Pea as she mended her raft. She tied it to a barge loaded with big boxes of Bunny Buns.

When a carton 'accidentally' fell overboard, she helped herself.

Day after day Sweet Pea floated lazily along under cool cloudy skies

as the other boats rushed up and down the river.

Then one morning the sun came out. "I think I feel warm!" said Sweet Pea. "THIS must be SOUTH!"

She steered her raft into a small cove and hopped off.
Sweet Pea wiggled her toes in the soft warm sand.

That night Sweet Pea feasted on her favorite foods...

then snuggled under
her fluffy puffy quilt.

She spent seven sunny spring days on the sand swimming, sleeping and sipping lemonade...

...until one night she had a dream and woke up lonely.

Sweet Pea packed up her boat, waited for a brisk breeze,

and sailed back up the river.

When the wind changed direction, she had to paddle, push and pull her boat along.

SPLISH SPLOSH

It was **not** an enjoyable journey anymore.

Finally, on a blustery spring day, Sweet Pea rounded the last bend in the stream.

She tied her boat, ran up the path and BURST through the door.

This is what she saw.

"Well," said Sweet Pea, "Time to plant my garden."

And she hoed a row in the sweet, soft soil.

About the Author Illustrator

Like a river, every story has a source. Marcia Leiter has hiked up mountains, floated down rivers, and camped on pine needles under the stars. She has also gotten soggy wet in the rain. This tale was written after returning from an adventurous winter voyage on southern seas. A jungle river, paddling on water and falling into it, birds, sunshine, feasting and a beach were involved. Any resemblance between the characters and actual people is merely coincidental. Bon voyage!

MAKE AN ORIGAMI BOAT

Get a sheet of paper.
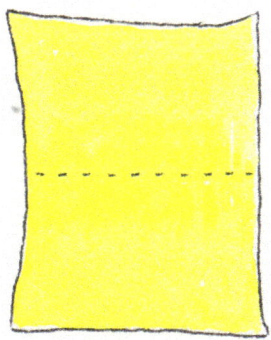

Fold it in half top to bottom.
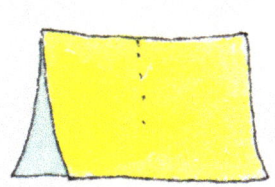

Crease it.

Open it. (center)
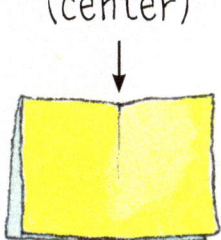

Fold upper left corner to the center.
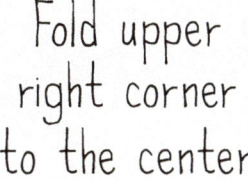

Fold upper right corner to the center.
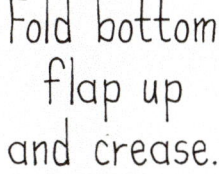

Fold bottom flap up and crease.

Turn over. Repeat.
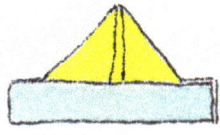

Pick it up. Push right and left edges together.

Rotate it. Tuck edge under

Turn over. Repeat.

Fold bottom corner to top.
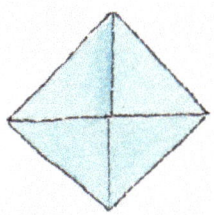

Turn over. Repeat.

You have a triangle.

Push right and left corners together. Rotate it.
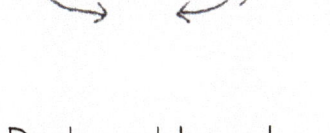
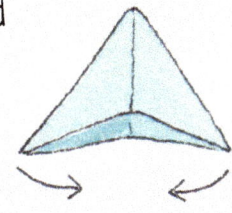

Pull tips out
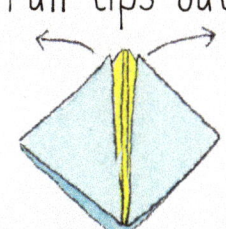

Form into boat. Float it!

'I SPY' TRAVEL GAMES
for 1 or more travelers

Look out the window and hunt for each of these.

SOMETHING THAT IS...

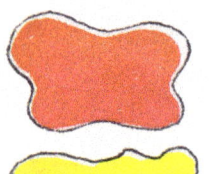 Red   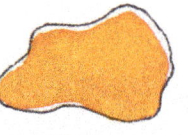 Orange   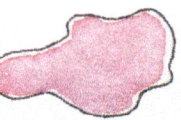 Pink
 Yellow    Green    Black
 Blue   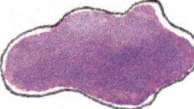 Violet    White
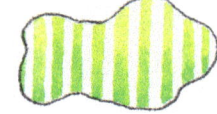 Striped 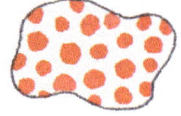 Spotted  Gray

SOMETHING SHAPED LIKE...

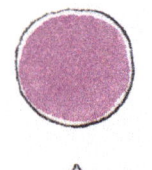  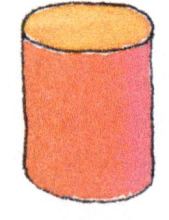  

   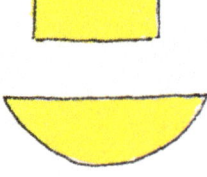 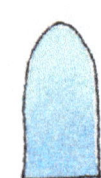

Something starting with: A B C D E F G H I J

How many of these can you spy?

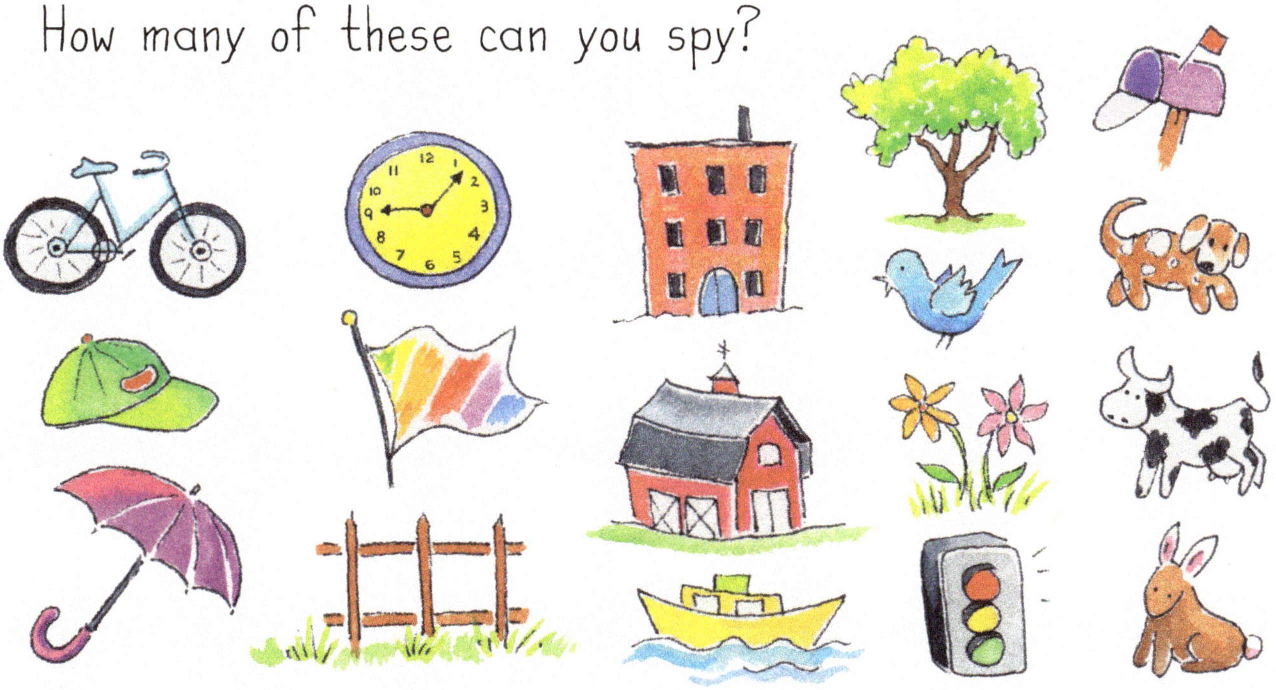

1 2 3 4 5 6 7 8 9 0 $

Try to find each of these types of road signs:

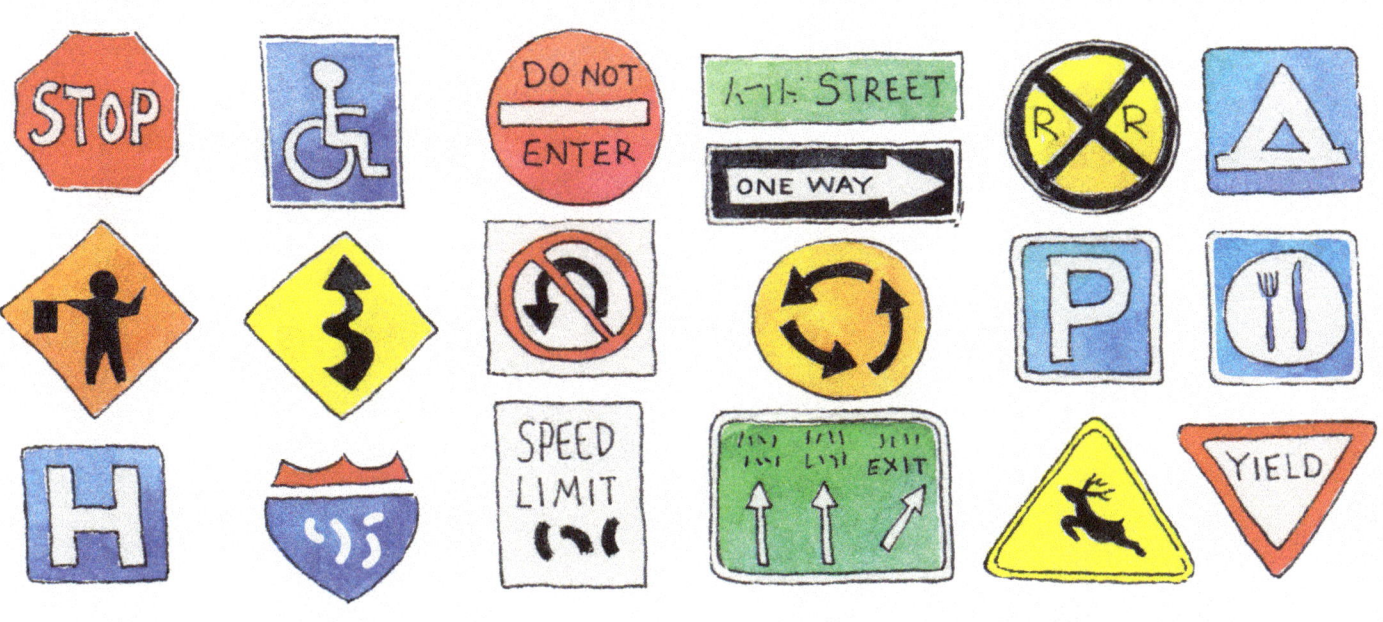

K L M N O P Q R S T U V W X Y Z

Sweet Pea's Journey SEEK  and  FIND

 A candy cane hat

A nest of squirrels

A mouse shoveling snow

 Asleep  on the job.

String Bean  upside down!

Tumbling  turnips

A stinky blue sock

A jelly-faced chipmunk

 A bride in white

A happy  mousefish

A very sharp  pencil

 A stray twinklefly

Help is on the way!!

A hungry  growly tum

 Buying bird seed

A helpful friendly snail

Paying for groceries

 Bugs in trouble!

 A frozen Ice Bunny

Acorns for dinner. YUM.

A bagel?  For fishie?

A polka dot  outfit

A proud papa frog

 A surfing mouse

Cowboy riding  a log?

 A pirate captain

Blue boxers and a belly

A puzzled  barge bunny

A nesting redbird

 House hunting

A piggy back  ride

Let go of my wing!

 Stuck in a pickle jar

Buried in the  sand

Nervous tightrope walker

String Bean's  house

 Uh oh! HELP!!!!!!!!

Watering the tulips

Playing with  nails?

 A whistling tea kettle

Munching on sweet peas

Home  sweet home

Starry starry night

 A book on the beach

A rocky bumpy  ride

Game's over! Now you can

CPSIA information can be obtained
at www.ICGtesting.com
Printed in the USA
LVHW071452131119
637243LV00019B/452/P